THEE GOBLIN LEGACY

By India Cunningham

Words 4,559

VARKA

"Varka – The Leader of Thee Goblin Legacy"

The History of the Goblins.

The goblins of *Thee Goblin Legacy* are not just creatures of myth, they are a people with a rich history, deeply rooted traditions, and a relentless drive for survival. Their culture is a fusion of ancient wisdom, warrior resilience, and a deep connection to craftsmanship and legacy. Goblins were once rulers of vast underground kingdoms, their cities carved from obsidian and stone, glowing with enchanted runes that told the stories of their past. They thrived in an era where supernatural beings coexisted with humans until fear and greed led to their near extinction. Centuries ago, powerful human factions, fearing goblin magic and influence, waged war against them, driving them into hiding. Their fortresses crumbled, their names were erased from history, and the goblins who survived were forced into the shadows, waiting for the right moment to reclaim their place in the world. Goblin society is built on loyalty, craftsmanship, and resilience. Each goblin has a role within their family or clan, and the hierarchy is based not only on strength but also on wisdom and contribution to their legacy.

The Matriarch: The leader, often the wisest and strongest, responsible for guiding the family through challenges. (*Varka embodies this role in the modern era.*)

The Strategists: Those who handle political moves, business dealings, and expansion efforts. (*Zyphra takes on this role in their new world.*)

The Protectors: Warriors and enforcers who ensure their survival. (*Dravok and Riven stand as their frontline defenders.*)

The Innovators: Artists, crafters, and builders who keep the culture alive through creation. (*Nessa and Gremm bring this aspect into modern business.*) Goblins do not believe in weakness, but their strength is not just in battle it is in adaptation. To survive the ages, they have had to reinvent themselves, blending into human society while keeping their traditions alive.

Goblin Craftsmanship

One of the most sacred aspects of goblin culture is craftsmanship. From weapons to jewelry, every piece a goblin creates tells a story. Their symbols and runes, passed down through generations, hold meanings of power, protection, and prosperity.

When Varka and her family decided to start *Thee Goblin Legacy*, they were not just building a business they were reviving a lost art, reclaiming their heritage, and proving that goblins still had a place in the modern world. Their designs are not just fashion; they are statements of survival, pride, and history.

The Struggle for Acceptance

Despite their resilience, goblins have never been fully accepted in human society. Myths paint them as monstrous, as creatures that should be feared or eradicated. *Thee Goblin Legacy* is their way of defying that narrative, proving that they are not just relics of the past they are forces of the present and the future. Some humans embrace them, intrigued by their history and culture. Others reject them, unwilling to accept their return. But goblins, as they have always done, stand unshaken. For goblins, history is not something to be forgotten. It is a weapon, a lesson, and a reminder that they are still here. And they always will be.

Chapter 1: Arrival in the Modern World

The city was alive with noise car horns blaring, neon lights flashing, and the constant chatter of humans rushing through the streets. It was overwhelming, chaotic, and completely different from the lands the goblins once ruled. Varka stood at the edge of a bustling sidewalk, her piercing emerald eyes scanning the towering glass buildings and the strange world before her. She adjusted the fur lined coat draped over her shoulders, the weight of her family's legacy pressing down on her as she turned to face the others. Stay close, she said firmly. Her siblings and Unk Durgen's son, Korvok, stepped forward, their presence drawing stares from humans who barely concealed their curiosity and their fear. Riven rolled her eyes. They act like they've never seen goblins before. They probably haven't, Gremm muttered, adjusting the sleek black suit he had insisted on wearing to blend in. His eyes gleamed with curiosity as he took in the neon signs and digital screens flashing advertisements. Dravok, always the silent observer, remained a step behind, watching the shifting expressions of the humans around them. The whispers were already starting. They don't belong here... Are they some kind of performers? "I heard they live underground like rats." A sneer curled at the corner of Riven's lips. Say that to my face, she growled under her breath, cracking her knuckles. Enough, Varka said sharply. We didn't come here to fight. Zyphra, always the one thinking ahead, stepped forward. We need a plan, Varka. If we're going to survive here, we need more than just our name we need power. And power, in this world, comes from influence. That was when Nessa, who had been silently taking in the sights, turned toward the massive LED billboard flashing above them. The screen showcased a popular fashion designer, parading their latest collection extravagant gowns and accessories, dripping in gold and jewels. Nessa's eyes flickered with inspiration. Then let's give them something they've never seen before. The others turned to her, curiosity piqued. A business, she continued. Our designs, our culture our legacy. If they won't accept us as we are, we'll make them want to. Unk Durgen scoffed; his arms crossed. And you think humans will buy goblin made things? Hah. They fear us, little one. They always have. Varka smirked, her sharp teeth glinting under the city lights. Then we'll make them see us differently. At that moment, the idea was born. The goblins weren't here to hide. They were here to build a legacy. And nothing human or otherwise was going to stop them.

Chapter 2: The Idea for Thee Goblin Legacy & Finding a Home

The old warehouse smelled of dust and forgotten history. It had been abandoned for years brick walls covered in graffiti, shattered windows letting in streaks of moonlight. Yet, to the goblins, it was full of possibility. Varka stepped into the center of the empty space, her boots echoing across the cracked floor. This will do, she declared, turning to the others. You're joking, right? Riven scoffed, arms crossed. This place looks like it survived a war. Exactly, Zyphra said, brushing her fingers along an old metal beam. Like us. Dravok remained silent, scanning the room for weak points, already assessing security risks. Korvok, always the most impulsive, kicked over an empty can. I like it. Feels...raw. Like us. We can make this into something big. Gremm pulled out his tablet, tapping rapidly. If we clean it up, modernize the front, and launch an online store, we could reach humans who don't fear us. People love exclusivity. We make our brand feel rare, high status, they'll buy it just to feel special, Zyphra finished, nodding. Nessa's mind was already racing with designs goblin culture woven into modern fashion, rings and necklaces imbued with ancient symbols, patterns humans had never seen before. Unk Durgen, who had remained quiet throughout, suddenly spoke. You're all fools. Silence fell over the group. Varka turned to him. Explain. The elder goblin sighed, shaking his head. You think selling trinkets and cloth will change how they see us? Bah. Humans fear what they don't understand. No brand will change that. We're not trying to change all of them, Zyphra said. Just enough to matter. Unk Durgen grunted but said nothing more. Riven smirked. So, what do we call this little empire of ours? Varka looked around at her family, each one of them standing strong despite the world against them. She let the words roll off her tongue like a promise. **Thee Goblin Legacy.** At that moment, their future was set. After securing their business location, there was still one more problem the goblins needed a place to call home. For centuries, they had lived in grand palaces, deep within mountains, or hidden in the forests of the old world. But here, in this human dominated era, there were no castles, no vast underground kingdoms. They had to settle for something...different. It was Zyphra who found the house. A three-story Victorian style manor abandoned but still standing strong. The paint was peeling, the garden overgrown, but the structure itself had presence. It sat on the edge of the city, far enough from human interference but close enough to keep watch over their growing enterprise. Standing before it, Varka exhaled slowly. It's not our palace, she admitted. No, it's not, Dravok agreed. But it will do. Riven kicked open the rusted gate, stepping onto the cracked stone pathway. I like it. Looks like it's been through hell, just like us. Nessa ran her fingers over the wooden carvings along the front door. The craftsmanship reminded her of their old home the delicate etchings, the history embedded in its walls. We can make it ours. Unk Durgen stood a few steps back, arms crossed. A home is more than wood and stone, he muttered. But I suppose we must start somewhere. Varka placed a hand on the door handle. Then let's start here. With a firm push, the door creaked open, revealing dust covered floors, grand staircases leading up to shadowed corridors, and forgotten memories lingering in the air. This wasn't a palace. But it was a beginning. And for now, that was enough.

Chapter 3: Building the Business

The house had barely been cleaned when the real work began. The goblins worked tirelessly day and night transforming the dusty warehouse into what would become *Thee Goblin Legacy.* Nessa was at the heart of it. In the evenings, she sat in their new home, sketching designs by candlelight, each stroke of her pen blending goblin culture with modern human fashion. She envisioned rings engraved with their ancient symbols, robes infused with their old-world style, and jewelry crafted from materials that once held magic. We have to make them want it, Zyphra said as she reviewed Nessa's work. Humans are drawn to power even if they don't understand it. We make our brand feel like a mystery, like something sacred. Gremm, already deep in research, nodded. We sell them a legacy, not just clothing. The problem was Goblins didn't exactly have connections in human society. Zyphra and Dravok handled the business side visiting human suppliers, negotiating deals, and sometimes intimidating those who tried to cheat them. In one tense meeting, a supplier looked at Zyphra with thinly veiled disgust. Goblins don't belong in this industry, he sneered. Dravok didn't say a word. He simply crushed a metal coin between his fingers and dropped the crumpled remains on the supplier's desk. After that, the supplier changed his tune. Gremm launched the online presence, knowing humans were obsessed with social media. Korvok, always eager to prove himself, began talking to street influencers and underground communities who loved anything rare and exclusive. Slowly, word began to spread. People started whispering about *Thee Goblin Legacy*. A brand unlike anything else. Fashion with mystery, power, and magic woven into its threads. A business ran by real goblins. And with attention...came trouble. One evening, as Riven was returning to the warehouse, she spotted a group of humans vandalizing their storefront. Filthy creatures don't belong here, one of them muttered, spray painting **GET OUT**! across the window. Riven's blood boiled. Without thinking, she stepped out of the shadows, her eyes glowing with fury. You got something to say? The group froze. One of them a man taller than her tried to stand his ground. Yeah. We don't want you freaks here. Riven cracked her knuckles. Then you should've left before I caught you. Before the humans could react, Dravok appeared behind them. The humans fled instantly, leaving behind their spray cans and shattered pride. Riven smirked, watching them run. Cowards, but the incident was a warning. Not everyone was happy about goblins stepping into the modern world. Some would try to stop them.

Chapter 4: Facing Rejection
Success was a double-edged sword.

At first, *Thee Goblin Legacy* started gaining real traction. Their unique designs, infused with the essence of goblin culture, caught the eye of humans who loved the unusual, the rare, the exclusive. Orders trickled in through their website, and small underground fashion circles began talking about the goblin owned brand that was changing the game. But with attention came resistance. The Protesters It started with whispers. Then the whispers became online hate. Then, one morning, they woke up to a full-fledged protest outside their shop. A group of angry humans stood outside, holding signs. **KEEP GOBLINS OUT! THIS IS A HUMAN WORLD! THEY DON'T BELONG HERE!** Varka stood at the entrance, arms crossed, watching the crowd. She didn't flinch, didn't move just stared them down like an empress looking upon fools. They fear what they don't understand, Zyphra muttered beside her. They need to fear something else, Riven growled. Me, she took a step forward, but Varka stopped her with a hand on her shoulder. Not yet. Inside the store, the family gathered. Dravok paced near the windows, watching the protesters with cold, calculating eyes. We need to shut this down before it escalates. They want a reaction, Zyphra said. If we fight them, we prove their point. Unk Durgen grunted from the corner; arms crossed. Told you. You thought you could be part of their world? This is what happens when goblins try to 'fit in. Silence hung in the air. Korvok clenched his fists. So, what do we do? Just let them run us out. No, Varka said. We do the opposite. She stepped toward the door, opening it slowly. The protesters turned their angry gazes on her. And she smiled. Ladies and gentlemen, she called out. Welcome to *Thee Goblin Legacy*. If you're here to learn about us, come inside. If not well, you're still giving us free publicity. Some of the humans hesitated, confused by her reaction. A few in the crowd shifted uncomfortably. One protester sneered. You don't belong here. Varka's smile widened, her sharp teeth gleaming. We do now. And with that, she turned and walked back inside, leaving the protesters fuming. Later that evening, when the protesters finally cleared, a man in a sharp gray suit entered the store. His presence immediately put Dravok on edge. Something about him was... off. You're making waves, the man said, looking around. I like that. Zyphra narrowed her eyes. And you are? He smirked, handing them a business card. **Alec Vaughn. CEO of Vaughn & Co. Investments.**

I see potential in your brand, Alec continued. With the right backing, you could go global. Imagine your designs in luxury stores, goblin made fashion on every high-end runway. Varka and Zyphra exchanged a glance. And what do you want in return? Varka asked. Alec's smirk grew wider. "Just a percentage. Control over branding, direction, public relations. Think of me as your bridge into high society. More like a leash, Dravok muttered. Alec chuckled. Come now. I'm offering you a future where humans welcome you, not protest you. Unk Durgen scoffed. You mean a future where we're your puppets. Alec ignored him, turning his gaze back to Varka. The way I see it, you have two choices. Struggle forever against human resistance... or let me make that resistance disappear. The room was silent. Everyone was waiting for Varka's decision. Her fingers brushed against the gold emblem on her coat an ancient symbol of their people. And then she spoke. No. Alec's smile faltered. No? We built this ourselves, she said. And we'll succeed ourselves. Alec studied her for a moment before his friendly expression darkened. Suit yourself, he said smoothly, tucking his card away. But don't be surprised when you find the world doesn't take kindly to your kind. He turned and walked out, leaving a heavy silence in his wake. That night, as the family sat around their grand dining table in their new home, Varka spoke. Things are changing, she said. We're not just building a business. We're challenging the world. And they don't like that. They'll try to stop us, Dravok said. They already are, Riven muttered. Then we'll do what we've always done, Unk Durgen said. He leaned forward, his old eyes sharp. We survive.

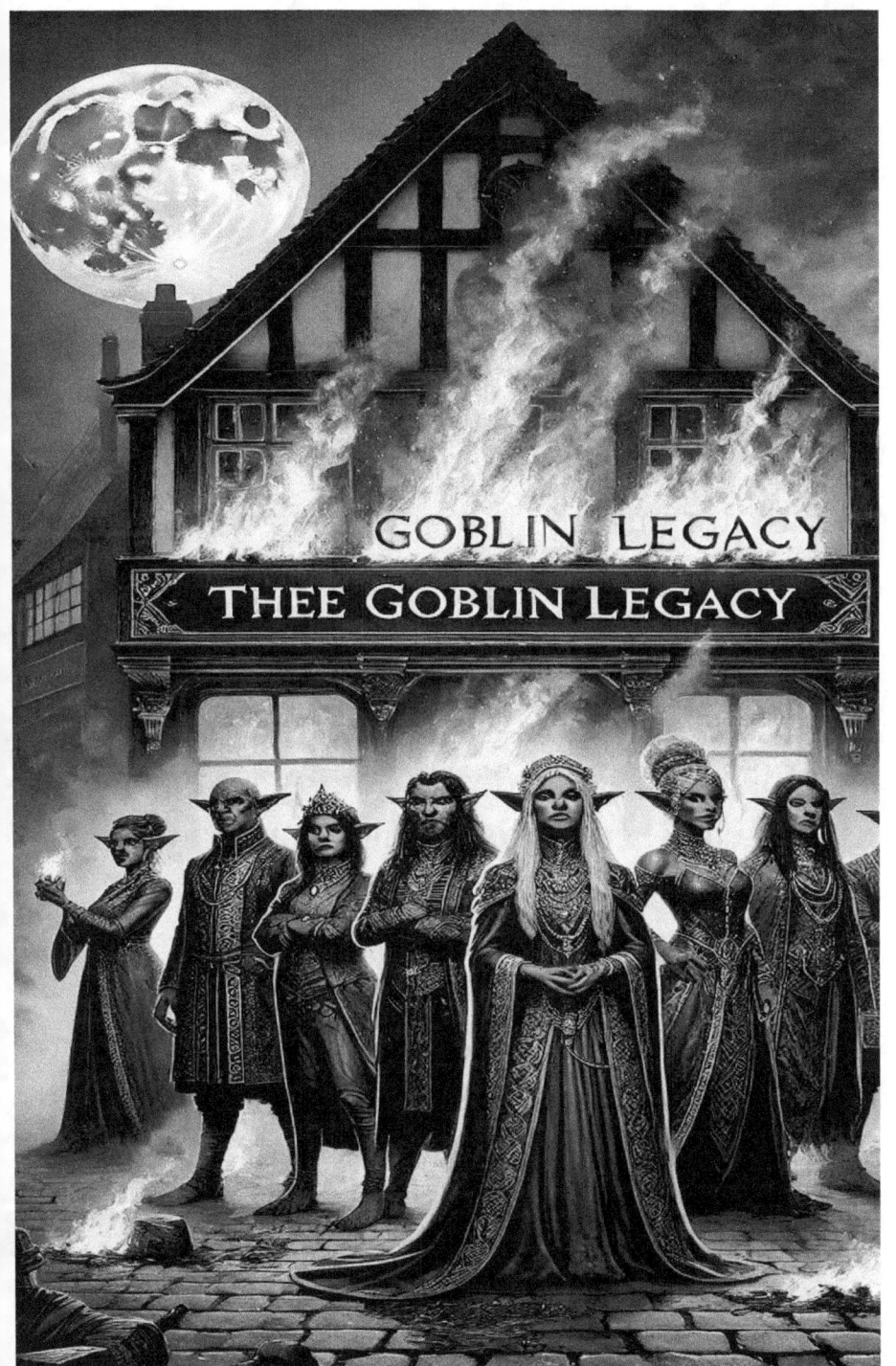

Chapter 5: A Betrayal & A Setback

The tension in the air was thick. The rejection from Alec Vaughn lingered like a storm cloud over *Thee Goblin Legacy*, but Varka refused to let it shake them. That was until everything came crashing down. It happened late at night. Dravok, always on high alert, heard the first crash. A bottle lit with fire smashed through the front window, flames licking at the edges of their store. Then another. By the time the family rushed outside, the entire front of Thee Goblin Legacy was ablaze. NO! Nessa gasped, her heart shattering at the sight of her carefully designed displays burning. Korvok clenched his fists. This wasn't random. Varka's eyes darkened. This was a message. Riven was already scanning the darkened streets, nostrils flaring. Let me track them. I'll find out who! No, Dravok interrupted, his gaze locked on the flickering flames. We already know. They all did. Alec Vaughn. This was what happened when you refused to fall in line. Someone On the Inside The fire wasn't the worst part. The next morning, while shifting through the damage, Zyphra made a chilling discovery. The security system had been disabled from the inside. It had to be someone with access, she said, scanning the list of people who had access codes. Only family had those codes. A heavy silence fell over the room. You're saying... one of us? Nessa whispered, unable to believe it. Varka's jaw tightened. No! Someone close, but not family. Gremm's eyes flickered with realization. Our assistant. Lior! The young goblin they had trusted to help run the shop. The one who had always seemed eager to be part of the family. The one who had disappeared the night before. Tracking Lior down wasn't hard. Dravok and Riven found him in a sleek downtown hotel, living far beyond his means. He had been paid off. Tell me why I shouldn't break every bone in your body, riven snarled, grabbing him by the collar. Lior's eyes darted around the room, desperate. I had no choice! he sputtered. Alec Vaughn, he offered me security. He said you we're all doomed anyway! I had to think about my own survival! Coward! Dravok leaned in, voice dangerously low. And what else did he tell you? Lior swallowed hard, then spoke the words that changed everything. Alec Vaughn... he's not human. Silence! What? Varka's voice was calm, but her fists were clenched. Lior's eyes darted between them. He's not human. He he's something else. Something old. That's why he wanted to control you. He doesn't just want your business he wants your bloodline gone. A slow, chilling realization washed over them. *Alec Vaughn hadn't just been trying to shut them down. He was something deeper, older.* An enemy, and now... war was coming.

Chapter 6: The Fight for Their Future
Alec Vaughn had declared war.

The fire at their store. The betrayal of Lior. The realization that Vaughn was not just a businessman, but something ancient, something that wanted them erased. Now, it was time to fight back. Zyphra and Gremm took to the digital world, digging through records that no human should have access to. They found something chilling. Alec Vaughn wasn't just a powerful investor. His name had existed for centuries. Different identities. Different business empires. But always the same face. This isn't just some human with a grudge, Zyphra muttered. He's something else. Gremm's fingers flew across the keyboard. He hacked into Vaughn's private files. What he found made his blood run cold. He's part of an ancient order, Gremm said. A secret faction of old-world elites that have been working to erase nonhuman bloodlines for centuries. He doesn't just hate us. He's made it his mission to wipe us out. The room went silent. Varka's gaze was unreadable. Then she spoke. Then we end him first. The Hunt Begins Riven and Dravok didn't wait. Tracking down Vaughn's allies, enforcers, and corrupt officials, they took the fight directly to those who had tried to bring *Thee Goblin Legacy* down. One by one, they eliminated threats. A corrupt police captain found unconscious in his car, career ruined. A corporate partner funding Vaughn's operation bank accounts drained, reputation shattered. A group of humans who had vandalized their store terrified into silence. But Vaughn himself! Still untouchable. Until a message arrived! A letter! From Alec Vaughn. You think you can fight me? Meet me. Let's settle this the right way. A challenge. The family gathered around the grand dining table. The room was filled with tension. He's daring us to walk into a trap, Dravok said. Which means he's either arrogant or desperate, Zyphra added. Unk Durgen, silent for most of the conversation, finally spoke. You can't fight this man like he's just another enemy. He's something older, something that plays by a different set of rules. Varka nodded slowly. Then we change the game. She stood, eyes fierce. We go to the meeting. Shock rippled through the room. You want to walk into Vaughn's hands? Korvok asked, disbelief in his voice. We go, Varka repeated, but we go prepared. They wouldn't just survive. They would win, and *Thee Goblin Legacy* would not fall.

Chapter 7: The Showdown
The meeting was set.

Alec Vaughn had chosen a high-rise penthouse in the city as the location a symbol of his power, his control. But what he didn't know was that the goblins weren't coming unprepared. The Walk into the Lion's Den Dressed in their finest battle-ready attire, the goblins arrived at the building. Not as victims. Not as beggars. But as a family that had survived centuries. Varka led the way, her long coat sweeping behind her. Riven and Dravok flanked her, both tense, ready. Zyphra and Gremm stayed close, their minds working on every possible way out. Nessa, calm but sharp, observed everything. Korvok eager but controlled was the last to enter. Security didn't dare stop them. They rode the elevator in silence. Each of them knew this wasn't just about *Thee Goblin Legacy* anymore. This was about survival, and then, the elevator doors opened. The penthouse was pristine, elegant, soulless. A wall of windows overlooked the city, and at the center of the room, Alec Vaughn stood waiting. He was still in his signature gray suit, but now, the facade was gone.

His eyes glowed with an unnatural light something inhuman, ancient. His skin seemed too perfect, too smooth, as if it barely held together something far worse beneath. You came, Vaughn said, smiling. Varka stepped forward. You wanted a meeting. Here we are. Alec studied them, his amusement growing. You truly don't understand, do you? And then, before their eyes he changed. His form stretched, his skin cracked. The perfect human exterior peeled away, revealing something monstrous beneath. A creature older than goblins. Older than humans. omething that had existed in the shadows of power for centuries. The fight exploded instantly. Dravok lunged first, his blade slicing through the air only for Vaughn to vanish, reappearing behind him. Riven attacked next her speed unmatched but Vaughn caught her fist mid strike, twisting her wrist with inhuman strength. You're strong, he said, grinning. But not strong enough. Gremm and Zyphra worked together hacking into the building's power grid, shutting off the lights, tilting the odds in their favor. But Vaughn wasn't just a man. He moved in the darkness like he was born in it. Then a scream. Korvok was thrown across the room, crashing into a marble table. Nessa whispered an ancient goblin incantation, summoning a burst of energy that finally forced Vaughn back. Varka didn't hesitate. She lunged forward; her dagger aimed for

Vaughn's throat. For the first time, Vaughn looked surprised. The blade pierced his skin. His form shuddered, flickering between monster and man. But then he laughed. You think you can kill me? he hissed, grabbing Varka by the throat. The family froze. And then Unk Durgen stepped forward. The elder goblin, who had warned them all along, now faced Vaughn directly. You think goblins are weak, Unk Durgen said, voice steady. You think we should have died out long ago. Vaughn sneered. Because you should have. Unk Durgen smiled. And then he spoke an ancient name. A name so old, so powerful, it made Vaughn recoil. The room trembled. A pulse of pure goblin energy erupted from Unk Durgen, wrapping around Vaughn, binding him in ways he couldn't break. Vaughn screamed, his form collapsing inward, his body disintegrating into nothing. The battle was over. Unk Durgen fell to his knees. The family rushed to him. You old fool, Varka muttered, her hands gripping his shoulders. Unk Durgen smiled, weary but victorious. I told you, He whispered. We survive.

Chapter 8: The Aftermath & The Future

The battle was over, but the war wasn't.

By the time the goblins left the penthouse, news had already spread. Rumors of what happened of a powerful man disappearing, of a confrontation between goblins and something unknown had begun circulating in both human and supernatural circles. Some feared them. Some respected them, but now everyone knew their name. Thee Goblin *Legacy* was no longer just a business, it was a movement. The family returned to their store, still damaged from the fire, still carrying the scars of Vaughn's attack, but they rebuilt. The first customers came in cautiously. Then more followed. The protests! Gone. The threats! Silenced, and in their place, Thee Goblin *Legacy* became an empire. Their designs weren't just clothing anymore. They were symbols of defiance, power, survival. Goblins, creatures of the old world, thriving in the new. But something was wrong. Unk Durgen had won the battle, had spoken a name that erased Alec Vaughn from existence. But it had changed him. His once steady hands now trembled. His once sharp eyes now glowed faintly, as if he had glimpsed something beyond this world. One night, as Varka sat with him, he spoke words that sent a chill through her bones. Vaughn was just a piece of something bigger, he whispered. Varka stiffened. What do you mean? Unk Durgen turned to her, and in his gaze was something old, something haunted. They're coming! The next morning, a letter arrived at their doorstep. The envelope was sealed with an unfamiliar symbol one none of them recognized. Varka opened it. Inside was a single sentence, written in a language older than even their kind. *You've made your move. Now it's our turn.* The family stared at the words. They had won the battle, but the war! It had just begun.

The End

www.ingramcontent.com/pod-product-compliance
Lightning Source LLC
Chambersburg PA
CBHW071604180626
46819CB00002B/124